Dear Child

John Farrell
Illustrated by Maurie J. Manning

Boyds Mills Press
Honesdale, Pennsylvania

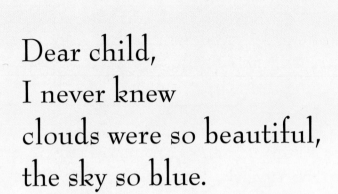

Dear child,
I never knew
clouds were so beautiful,
the sky so blue.

Leaves are much greener now.
More flowers in bloom,
strangers start smiling
when I tell them of you.

Birds' songs are sweeter,
each note rings clear.
The moon's light is brighter now
all because you are here.

How is this possible?
How can it be
that such a small child
has done this to me?

I hoped and I prayed
as we waited for you.
And then finally one day
all our wishes came true.

Dear, darling child,
you make me feel strong.
We dance without music.
We sing silly songs.

And it's you, dear child,
who have helped me to know
the thrills of ice-skating,
the wonders of snow.

How is this possible?
How can it be
that such a small child
has done this to me?

Dear child,
you made time stand still.
I loved you that moment,
and I always will.

Dear, sweet child,
you taught me to fly.
I find my wings
when I look in your eyes.

And together we'll learn
to look and to see
the stars in the sky
and the buds on the trees.

How is this possible?
How can it be
that such a small child
has done this to me?

Dear child,
I never knew
clouds were so beautiful,
the sky so blue.

Dear, sweet child,
you make time stand still.
I love you this moment,
and I always will.

So wherever you go
and whatever you do,
remember, dear child,
my love will go with you.

In memory of Mom, Gladys Buck Farrell,
who dearly loved each of her eighty-eight
children, grandchildren, and great-grandchildren

And to Lindsay Bates, for the inspiration
—J.F.

For Taavi, the youngest
—M.J.M.

Text copyright © 2008 by John Farrell
Illustrations copyright © 2008 by Maurie J. Manning
All rights reserved
Printed in China
Designed by Kelley Cunningham
First edition

Library of Congress Cataloging-in-Publication Data
Farrell, John.
Dear child / by John Farrell ; illustrated by Maurie J. Manning.
p. cm.
Summary: Illustrations of diverse families and simple text show
how children affect their loved ones for the better.

ISBN 978-1-59078-495-2 (hardcover : alk. paper)
[1. Family—Fiction. 2. Parent and child—Fiction.
3. Stories in rhyme.] I. Manning, Maurie, ill. II. Title.

PZ8.3.F2297Dea 2008
[E]—dc22
2007018977

Boyds Mills Press, Inc.
815 Church Street
Honesdale, Pennsylvania 18431